Dear Lucas ~

Forever Florida ... Christmas 2013

Enjoy with Love

LuLu + TV

For Alfred and Sybil
MKL

To my family for their love and support
DLD

Published by CS4Kids, an imprint of *The Coastal Star.*
To follow future adventures of Rosie and her family, visit www.CS4Kidsbooks.com.

ISBN: 978-0-9910556-0-9

Rosie's Song

Deep beneath the ocean, but not too far from shore,
Rosie lives along the reef's edge with soft sand
and seven busy brothers.

Her brother Quickstar is the speedy one, zipping along the coral reef with strong, long rays.

Astrostar and Apex are brave and curious, climbing high to peek above the waves.

The youngest boys are always laughing.
They are Rosie's favorites.

Copperstar tickles Rosie just to make her laugh.

And Harry practices magic tricks,
pulling shiny seashells from behind her tiny ears.

Known far and wide as Rover,
the oldest brother is a happy wanderer.

He's not like Wallstar,
who prefers to stay near home mixing tasty meals of mollusks.

Each night as the sun fades, the eight little sea stars say "good night."
They touch the tips of their rays to float together
as the sea breathes in and out across their sandy home.

Every morning, Rover, Quickstar, Apex and Astrostar wave goodbye
as they head off over the reef wall and out into the ocean.

Harry and Copperstar follow close behind,
searching for clown fish to learn a few new jokes.

Of the brothers, only Wallstar stays behind,
slicing seaweed in his comfy cave beneath the brilliant coral.

Out in the sand alone, Rosie stretches her rays and dreams of the day when she, too, can explore the endless ocean.

"Someday soon, I'll be a big sea star."

On this particular morning, something unusual happens:

The water fills with bubbles!

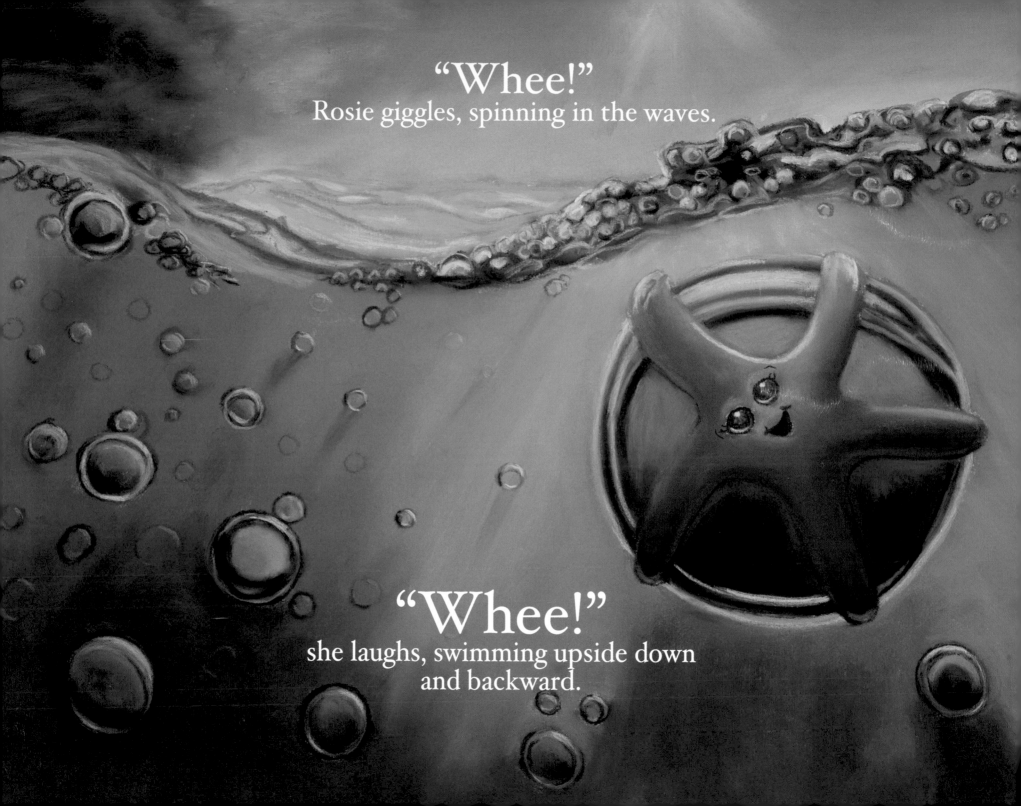

"Whee!"
Rosie giggles, spinning in the waves.

"Whee!"
she laughs, swimming upside down
and backward.

"Whee!"

she yells again...

... until one rough tumble
pushes her against sharp coral.

"Ouch,"
she cries,
clinging to the bumpy wall.

"This must be a storm," she thinks as the water grows cold and dark and the waves grow stronger.

Alone and scared, she begins to cry, her tears swept away in the surging sea.

Afraid that she might lose her grip,
Rosie begins to inch her way down
the jagged coral wall.

Then, through the deafening roar
of crashing waves she hears,

"Rosie? Is that you?"

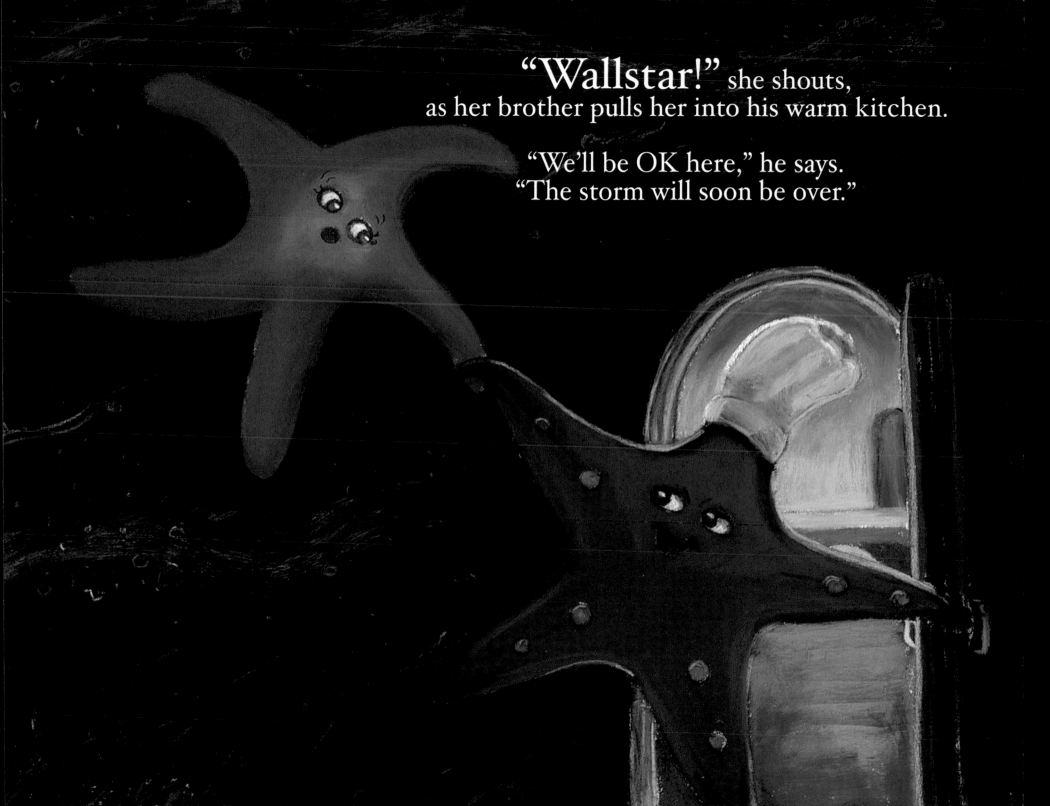

"Wallstar!" she shouts,
as her brother pulls her into his warm kitchen.

"We'll be OK here," he says.
"The storm will soon be over."

"Where are the others?" Rosie asks.
"They'll be fine," Wallstar says. "They are brave and strong and clever."

"But what if they're hurt?
What if they've been hit by a boat,
or have lost a ray and can no longer swim?
What if they're trapped in poisonous tentacles?"

"What if, what if, what if..." Wallstar sighs.

"What if they've been
eaten by a shark?"

"Don't be afraid, baby sister.
Help me cook some savory stew
and we'll wait for the storm to pass."

Rosie agrees to stir the pot
as Wallstar adds a dash of peppery
plankton and begins to sing:

Sea star shimmer, sea star shine
I'll be yours and you'll be mine
Together we will float and sway
And should we ever swim away
We will never be alone
Since we are family, we are
home.

In the morning, Rosie peeks outside the cave
as bits of broken boardwalks and boats rush past.

"I'll go and find the others now," Rosie vows,
as she peers through the dangerous debris.

"I don't think that's wise," Wallstar cautions.
"The ocean is still dangerous."

"I don't care," Rosie says.
"I'll search and search and search and bring them all back home."

"Your brothers have been through other storms," Wallstar says.
"They'll smell the simmering stew and find their own way home."

"But what if they don't?"
Rosie says.
"*You* can stay and cook,
but *I* will go and find them!"

Turning away, she shoots out the
door and into the unsettled sea.

"Be safe,"
Wallstar whispers,
as he watches her swim away.

Out in the ocean,
everything is all mixed up.

"Which way is the surface?"
Rosie wonders as she swims in circles.
"How do I know which way is the
shore and which way is the deep?"

Rosie's afraid when she bumps
into hard and scary things,
but she keeps swimming
and searching.

When her rays become tangled in floating fishing line,
she thrashes in panic, then takes a deep breath and wiggles her way free.

Frightened but determined, Rosie keeps swimming until she finds herself near the clear, warm water of the shore.

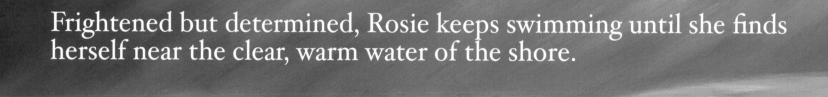

"I'll rest now," she says, and settles her aching rays into the soft, comforting sand.

Whoosh!

Suddenly she is lifted from the water
and blinded by the midday sun.

"Look what I found!"
she hears a loud voice shout.

A young human holds Rosie.

"Look how pretty," the boy says,
marveling at her perfect pastel hue.

"What a beautiful sea star."

"I would love to keep you," he laughs
as he lifts her toward the sun.

"But maybe you have a family, like I do.
I'll bet they would miss you."

Terrified, Rosie attempts to shout,
"Yes, yes, yes!
Have you seen my brothers?"
but finds she can't speak in the open air.

"Please, please, please, let me go..."
she tries to whisper.

"OK," the boy says,
as if he'd heard her plea.
"I suppose you should
go back to the sea
and be with your family."

With that, he gently tosses Rosie
spinning and tumbling into the ocean.

Once under the water, she lets herself float on the current farther from the shore.

"Oh, Wallstar. I don't feel so brave and strong right now."

Exhausted and too tired to swim,
she begins to fall toward the ocean floor.

When she dares to open her eyes,
Rosie sees an amazing sight...

... a circle of sea stars floating far below.

As she nears the bottom, six brothers shout,
"Where have you been?"

"Where have *YOU* been?" Rosie laughs.

As her brothers rush to tell their tales of survival, Rosie stops them.

"Has anyone seen Rover?"

Her brothers look away and mumble, "No."

"Oh, no!" Rosie cries.

"What if he's lost?
What if he's wounded?
What if he's not coming home?"

Just then, Wallstar points toward the surface, "**Look!**" he shouts, "It's Rover!"

As Rover drifts slowly down, Rosie can see that he's weak and tired.

"Oh, poor Rover."

"Don't worry, Rosie,"
Rover says as he nears the bottom.
"I'll be fine. I just need rest...

... and some of Wallstar's cooking!"

Just then the smell of simmering stew
reaches Rosie's nose.

"You were right, Wallstar.
You are all brave and
strong and clever!"

"Just like you, baby sister, just like you."

Now safe beneath the ocean, but not too far from shore,
Rosie and her seven busy brothers touch their rays and begin to sing:

Sea star shimmer, sea star shine
I'll be yours and you'll be mine
Together we will float and sway
And should we ever swim away
We will never be alone
Since we are family, we are home.

There would be no Rosie if not for *The Coastal Star* masthead design by Bonnie Lallky-Seibert. And our little sea star would never have started on her journey without the encouragement of Tom Sand.

Along the way, several "Friends of Rosie" were kind enough to help fine-tune her journey: Antigone Barton, Amy Driscoll, Viola Gienger, Rochelle Gilken, Lu Lippold and Susan Spencer-Wendel.

Miraculously, Deborah LaFogg Docherty knew immediately how Rosie's world should look. Her artistic talent brought this story to life.

In the production kitchen, copy editing and book design were provided by Victoria Preuss and Jerry Lower.

When we needed to create an above-sea scene Harrison Calder proved to be an excellent model for kind and caring children everywhere.

And a million sea star kisses to my husband for being the best story-listener ever.

Many thanks to all.

— *Mary Kate Leming*

Mary Kate Leming is a former musician and librarian who has dabbled in filmmaking, screen-writing and Web content development. After more than 20 years of gainful employment as a research manager and editor at daily newspapers, she now co-owns and edits *The Coastal Star*. This is her first published book.

Deborah LaFogg Docherty's award-winning art combines her two great loves: nature and painting. Her favorite media are acrylics, oils and pastels (which were used for this book). Her paintings have been featured in museum shows, national and international art shows, books and magazines. This is the second children's book she has illustrated. For more information about her art and events, please go to www.lafogg.com.

Both Leming and LaFogg Docherty live near the soft sand of the Florida shore. Reach them at Rosie@CS4Kidsbooks.com